152 Brooks

Cheryl D. Nash

INFINITY
PUBLISHING.COM

ISBN 0-7414-5788-1

Published by:

INFINITY PUBLISHING.COM

1094 New DeHaven Street, Suite 100
West Conshohocken, PA 19428-2713
Info@buybooksontheweb.com
www.buybooksontheweb.com
Toll-free (877) BUY BOOK
Local Phone (610) 941-9999
Fax (610) 941-9959

Printed in the United States of America

Published March 2010

152 Brooks

At first he didn't notice, then it grew too conspicuous not to be noticed. He didn't know any of the neighbors because he was new in the neighborhood. Harry Cromwell was your average, everyday guy, who would have never dreamed of such a thing happening to him, but it did.

It all started when he moved from his former residence to a small, convenient house on Brooks Avenue. He was aware of the house next to his at first, but then he became more and more interested.

The first time he saw her, was the first night that he stayed in his new residence. It was a warm, still, muggy night, in which you toss and turn and never really go into a sound sleep. His bedroom window was open to let out the heat from the previous day. He lay still, hardly breathing, listening to the quietness, when that soft, still quietness was rudely interrupted by the sound of a woman's mocking, robust laughter. It floated on the night air with a resounding of echo upon echo. He thought it rather strange, since it was one o'clock in the morning. So, brushing the hair out of his eyes, he stumbled from the bed over to the window, where the warm night air felt hot against his face. At first he couldn't come in contact with the source of the laughter, but then he did spot the yellow, reddish glow of a candle, just as the laughter began once again. It projected from the top of the house, which resided next to his, where a tower like structure was built. Fortunately for him, there was a full moon that night, thus allowing him to view the scene much more accurately than was needed. She was tall, dark haired, and fair complected, with dark almost black eyes that reflected the image of the candle, which she held in her hand. Clutching it tightly she threw her head back, letting her hair slide away from her smooth, white shoulders, showing the bareness of skin while she laughed. Once more she looked down out of her window to the front lawn, whence her expression changed to that of horror. She fled in her white nightgown, while the light of the candle glowed along the opposite wall, slowly descending downward until every last ray blended in with the shadows.

He tried to put it out of his mind, what he had seen, but it just would not pass. It kept running through his mind like a silent picture show. It was a long while before the darkness washed away the visions, which danced in his head, then the sunlight took the place of darkness. It poured into his room leaving no corner unexposed. Funny how it all seemed a dream, but he knew that it wasn't. How to convince anyone that he wasn't dreaming, would be beyond his scope of persuasion. There was only one person he knew he could trust and felt that she would believe him, that was Cleo Thompson. They had recently met through friends and had become good friends.

At one time, Harry had wanted to be more than just friends with Cleo. He was definitely attracted to her. He liked her cleanliness and wholesomeness. He presented her with a gift, which she promptly refused. He felt crushed, hoping that she would feel the same way about him. She turned him down graciously. She explained to him that she felt only something akin to sisterly love for him and no more, that their relationship would go no further than friendship. She confessed to no physical attraction and did not wish to endanger their valuable friendship with a romantic interest. They had a lot in common and foolishly she thought he only viewed her as a good friend as well. What it all boiled down to was that romantically he just wasn't her type. It was then he discovered rejection's cruel sting. He in turn had done the same in the past. He should have been more tactful and gentle in his reaction to the proposed action.

Thinking about Cleo he suddenly remembered that he hadn't called her since he finished moving. He did invite her over to see the house once he was settled. Not today, perhaps another time, he felt like a caged lion and just wanted to get out in the open for awhile. Promising to phone Cleo after breakfast, he put his conscious to rest. His room seemed so gay that he didn't hesitate to get up and start the regular, morning routine.

"Hello. Oh hi, Harry. No I'm not busy for lunch. How about if I come over to see the house?"

"Well, I'd rather come over to your place. You can see the house some other time."

"Harry, what's wrong? Don't you remember how anxious you were to have me come over and see the house as soon as possible?"

"Ya, I know, but all that has changed now. I just want to get out of the house for awhile."

"But Harry, you've only been there one night, haven't you?"

"Yes, but I said that I wanted to get out of the house for awhile, that's all!"

"Well, you don't have to get snappy. If there is something bothering you…Harry?… Harry?" He certainly did feel like getting out of the house, that was true, but explaining his feelings was never easy for him. After all, he didn't even know where to start.

Quickly he locked the door and headed for the garage, but he stopped once, just once, to look at the house, which resided next to his, 152 Brooks. Perhaps it was his eyes playing tricks on him, but he could swear that he saw the curtain move in one of the upstairs windows.

How good it felt to be in the quiet sanctuary of his car and not the enclosed surroundings of the house, where it seemed he had spent a very long time. He backed the car out of the garage. A tingling chill shot up his back and down his arms, as he backed down the driveway. The very strong heat and light of the sun seemed blotted out, as if it had turned into a cold, gray stone, which didn't belong where it had once shone down upon 152 Brooks. Last night, after his strange encounter, he climbed back into bed and pulled the covers up tightly around himself. He needed to keep out the dead, still cold, which had crept into his room following him as he retreated from the window. It stabbed at him with its fingers and tried to find an opening in the covers, where it could sneak in. It frightened him to realize how much this little incident had bothered him, but it did. Why should it bother him? If he could have answered that question, he would have felt much better.

He arrived at Cleos where lunch was neatly set out on the patio for two.

"Well, now that you're here, shall we eat? I'm starved!"

"Is everything ready?"

"Sure is. You know you sounded awfully uptight over the phone. Is there something bothering you? Maybe you would like to talk about it!"

"I really wouldn't want to burden you with my problems."

“You wouldn’t be burdening me, after all what are friends for?”

“I was hoping that I would come up with a good explanation by the time that I got here. I haven’t got one yet, so I’ll tell it like it is.”

“Go ahead. I’m all ears.”

“That’s what I was afraid of. I’ve never really been bothered by something of this sort before and that’s what really upsets me! Anyway, yesterday afternoon I finally finished moving in. I had everything set up where I wanted it. Once I was done I relaxed for the rest of the evening, till I decided to turn in for the night. I really couldn’t sleep too soundly because of the heat.”

“I know what you mean. The heat makes it hard to sleep. It sure is a blessing if you have an air conditioner.”

“I woke up around one in the morning, some woman was laughing hysterically just outside my bedroom window. I got up to look and saw a woman in the tower window of the house next to mine. She was holding a candle and laughing. She looked haunting. You know what I mean?”

“In what way? Was she disfigured?”

"No. I don't mean that she was ugly enough to scare me. In fact, she was very beautiful. It was just the expression on her face. She laughed a couple of times and then a look of fear sprang upon her face. She turned and left just as suddenly as she had come. After that, I had a chill that lasted all night. Things seemed better this morning, everything looked ordinary. I was actually freezing until I got in the car to come here. Sorry if I got snappy over the phone, but I just needed to get out of the house for awhile. You can understand what I'm trying to say?"

"I will admit there have been times when I have felt the same way. If I were you Harry, I'd just forget the whole thing. You were half awake and half asleep and in that state things seem to be magnified and stay with you longer, just like a bad dream."

"But, it wasn't a dream!"

"Don't be on the defensive. I didn't say that it was a dream, now did I? I believe you Harry! You don't lie, but you mustn't let your imagination run away with you."

"I guess you're right. I won't give it another thought. You always come up with the right solution."

"Elementary, my dear Harry, elementary. Would you like to go shopping with me after lunch?" The afternoon went by quickly and before they knew it they were eating dinner. Harry offered Cleo the chance to join him for a movie. He wanted to stay away from the house as long as possible.

It was a bright moonlight night, the second full moon in a row. He pulled his car into the garage and locked the door. The shadows of the trees stretched out their branches, as if to touch something alive. Of course, it is true that trees are living things, but they can't reach our standard of what is literally alive. They can't walk, talk, or think for that matter. He realized this also while walking up to the front door. He tried not to look, but he just couldn't keep himself from doing so. In the tower window, an oil lamp was burning brightly with the window open, to let in the fresh, cool night air. It had been a hot day. He turned to unlock the front door, but was in the midst of it when he heard a sort of squeaking sound. Turning around once again, he saw that the tower window had been closed and the shade drawn. Only thin lines of light were visible around the edges of the shade. He thought it rather strange that there were never any cars in the driveway, that the mailman never stopped at the house that, there were never any visitors, and above all there seemed to be no life in the house at all during the day.

The minute that he got inside, he went over to the stove to make some coffee. He planned to stay awake as long as possible, for sleep would come soon enough. He had two cups of coffee and then decided to watch a bit of television. An hour or so must have gone by, for he heard the clock strike twelve. He must have fallen asleep during the news for now, the feature movie was on the air. For a moment, he thought that he was dreaming, but realized all too quickly that he wasn't. The television went dead with the sound of the voices going slowly down the scale, at the same time the lights went out. He thought that he had blown a fuse, so sat there trying to remember approximately where he had put the flashlight. It was during this concentration that he suddenly heard the silence. Only the crickets and tree toads could be heard. At first he could hardly hear it, then he thought that someone was playing the radio, then the words were brought into distinction. It was a woman's voice, soft and sweet.

"Oh Harry, I've waited so long! Oh Harry, Harry, Harry…" Whoever or whatever it was then laughed slowly and gleefully. I guess you could call it instinct, for the next minute Harry was over at the window just in time to see the light in the tower window go out.

"Goodnight my love!" Next he smelled the strong, encompassing odor of lilac. It was as potent as smelling salts, as if it had been worn for hundreds of years, then it was gone as quickly as it had come. He staggered into the kitchen with a blank mind, to have just one last cup of coffee. He didn't want to retire, but he decided that what he had just experienced couldn't be any worse than a nightmare. Funny how he couldn't think about what just happened, but his hand still shook as he poured the coffee and wiped the sweat from his brow. The window would remain shut, this he had decided even before night fell.

He drifted off to sleep quickly, which was rather surprising. You could say that he was rather content, for he thought himself free of her for the rest of the night, but he was wrong, as he would soon see. For the first couple hours of sleep, he didn't dream at all.

Then the faces slowly grew into place, piece-by-piece, bit-by-bit, until he recognized them. Well, at least one of them, from which he recoiled in horror. It was her all right, but there were others also.

"Father must you really go? Is it all that important?"

"I'm afraid so dear. I shan't be gone long, only a week or two. Besides you're old enough to take care of yourself. The servants will keep you company and look after you as well."

"But, you know how lonely I get staying in this house day and night. It's all your fault. Why won't you let me go out? Why? Will you give me one good reason and tell me why? Please!"

"I told you never to bring that up again. I have my reasons. Now we must be going or I shall be late for my train and may miss it."

"You didn't answer my question. Why won't you let me have friends? Do you know what all the people in town call us? Do you really want to know? Well, I can tell you. Even though you never let me out of the house alone, I still can hear everything that they say about me, about us."

"I don't care what they call us or what they may say about us. We still have our pride and dignity, also our good family name to stand behind us. Besides, it doesn't matter what they think. It's what we think about ourselves that counts. Is that clear young lady?"

"Yes. In fact, it's too clear because I'm starting to think the same thing about us as they do." All words stopped at this point, tension floated in the air, and tempers flared. It must have been her father that she was talking to, for she resembled him in some ways. She was really quite beautiful, then. She hadn't aged a day, perhaps she hadn't.

Her father grabbed his coat and walked out the door, probably to restrain his dominant temper, which he could lose quite easily. He was a very tall, stern man with grayish, white hair. His physical features were darkened with age and wisdom. He entered a carriage and was soon joined by his daughter. The distance they drove was spent in silence, not even so much as a glance in the others direction.

Once they reached the train station, they both returned a hasty goodbye.

"Oh, excuse me. I wasn't watching where I was going."

"No that's quite alright. Actually it was my fault. It was I who wasn't watching where I was going."

"That wouldn't be proper for me to accept an apology from such a pretty girl. In fact, I refuse to accept it! You must accept mine."

"Why that's very kind of you! Please excuse me, but I must be going."

"Hey! Wait a minute. What are you doing for lunch? I have no special plans. Would you agree to join me?"

"I'm sorry, but I couldn't. You see father would not permit it."

"Who did you just see off on the train?"

"That was my father."

"Well, what he doesn't know won't hurt him, eh? Now where shall we have lunch?"

"My! You're the pushy type."

"Do you really think so? I've never noticed before."

"Funny too! Yes I'll have lunch with you." They picked a nice, little Italian restaurant.

"Why is it that you said your father wouldn't permit you to go with me?"

"Well, he's very set in his own ways. He hardly ever lets me go out of the house or have any friends. When I ask him why, he won't tell me. If he ever found me with you or anyone else, I'm afraid of what he might do. So please, don't bother to come and see me at the house. He might come back unexpectedly. If you want to see me, we will have to meet somewhere, like we're doing now. Understand?"

"Don't worry, you made that perfectly clear. Besides I wouldn't want to walk around with a hole in me from your father's shot-gun."

"I guess I was right, you are funny! Knowing my father, that is exactly what he would do."

"By the way, where do you live?"

"Over on Brooks Avenue."

"Which house?"

"The red and gray one, 152 Brooks." They went together numerous times during the two-week span that her father was absent. This Harry also dreamt, but only very briefly.

Harry woke up late the next morning. He had planned on storing away some of his belongings, that he wasn't using up in the attic. While finishing breakfast, he remembered that he hadn't gotten his mail yesterday.

"Say, you're my new neighbor, right? I'm David Garrison. How do you do?"

Harry turned and found himself facing a young man in his twenties. He was dressed very smartly to point out his physical attributes.

"Very well, thank you. I'm glad to meet you. I don't know many people around here."

"Yes, it was that way when I first moved here myself, but I finally got acquainted with everyone when I was invited to a party. Hey! That reminds me, I'm having a party tonight. Would you like to come? I'd be delighted to have you and I'm sure everyone else would also. Please do come!"

"I might at that. I don't have anything else planned for tonight. What time is it?"

"About nine o'clock."

"Good I'll be there." The only reason why he decided to go was to get out of the house. If he was lucky, the party would last till one or two in the morning. He really didn't like parties, but anything was better than having to sit at home and listen for noises. After the peculiar dreams he was having, he rather dreaded going to sleep at night. Yet at the same time, he looked forward to the unexpected. It seemed as if the essence of her presence would last forever.

He was lucky that there was plenty of storage space in the attic, he thought to himself as he carried a box up. He wouldn't have to cram all the stuff he wanted to store into his surrounding living space. The atmosphere of the attic caused his mind to wander to a different realm of thought. Could houses really be haunted? Were ghosts real? Perhaps this house had a resident ghost of it's own. That could explain all the weird experiences he had been having since he moved in. It would be easier to perform an exorcism than to move out. It took him a few months to find this place for rent. He was locked into a lease and didn't want any legal repercussions from moving out before the lease was up. Perhaps she would go away and leave him alone, but he instinctively knew that she wouldn't. Even now during the day, with the heat of the sun, he felt cold and the fixed stare of eyes upon him, though he was all-alone. The attic was still, dark, and musty. He would have to remember to bring a flashlight up with him the next time he brought boxes up. He opened the windows and stood in the breeze created. It would be hard work carting all of the boxes upstairs, but it must be done. He put the box down as far back as space allowed. A shadowy shape caught his eye. He couldn't quite determine what it was and had to crawl towards it on his hands and knees, careful not to bump his head on the ceiling joists, or give a home to an unwanted splinter. Apparently, someone had left a box of their belongings behind.

He really didn't want to invade another person's belongings, but he just had to see what was in the box. It turned out that the box was only half full. It contained a variety of pipes, tobacco, and a tablet of paper full of notes by a Doctor Harris. He wasn't very interested in the notes, but figured he would read them over anyway. Dr. Harris gave Harry the impression of being very distinguished, right down to the brand of tobacco he smoked. Harry settled back in his favorite chair, with a cup of coffee and started to read:

June 29, 1965: I just moved in and have finished adding final touches. I needed to get away from my all-defining profession. Of course, I chose to be a psychiatrist, but at times it can be both tiring and demanding. I have retired here for a short vacation. I picked a community where I wouldn't be known professionally. I plan to go over some of my recent cases, which needed my full attention.

June 30, 1965: Last night was my first night here. I didn't sleep too well because of the heat. Perhaps it was the heat, but I'm not entirely sure. At first I thought that I was having a nightmare, after all a man in my position who works under such strain, could have some of that stress rub off in his dreams. My feelings were so real that I can't be totally convinced that it didn't happen. All psychiatrists are taught to analyze feelings. The ones that I experienced were like no others that I have ever had before in my life. It must have been around one o'clock in the morning, when I heard a woman laughing. I arose, totally conscience of what was going on around me. Once I got to the window, I saw that it was coming from the top portion of the house next door. In the window there stood a most striking young lady, holding a candle and laughing. She stopped laughing and her facial expression changed to that of horror.

July 1-17, 1965: She appeared constantly, as if she were trying to tell me something. I don't think that she wanted to harm me, yet I can't help thinking that she wanted something from me. Once in awhile she would whisper a name. The name was Harry. I never expected to come across an apparition that was right next door. I hope that she may find rest for her soul, if not, then I am positive that she will not rest until she has accomplished her quest.

July 19, 1965: I am in the process of moving out. I have had a long enough vacation. I must be getting back to work, although I go back deeply troubled for that lost soul that roams tirelessly, and restlessly in 152 Brooks. There you have it, one of the many unsolved mysteries of the universe!

The last page was signed Dr. Harris. Harry could understand the appeal she has on those of the opposite sex. Most men feel the natural urge to help a damsel in distress. He wondered if there were any psychiatrists who helped the dead.

Harry picked up his cup, but discovered that it was empty. His mouth was dry and his eyes tired. He glanced at the clock. It was eight p. m., the party would be starting soon. He decided to take a shower, perhaps it would wash away his sleepiness.

"Well, it seems that I am the first one here."

"Don't worry about it, the others shall be arriving shortly. Come on in. Have a drink. What would you like?"

"Scotch if you don't mind."

"How long have you been in the neighborhood?"

"Oh about three days. By the way, have you met the girl that lives next door to me? 152 Brooks, I believe."

"A girl you say? That's news to me. I thought that I knew every girl in the neighborhood. Wait a minute, did you say 152 Brooks?"

"Ya, what about it?"

"Well, it seems that someone told me that the house was deserted. I was interested to know who lived there. They said that the house has been empty off and on for eighty-five years."

"Eighty-Five years? Wow! That's a long time. It doesn't look as if it is that old."

"I guess some guy owns it and has a cleaning woman come in once a week. What gave you the idea that someone lived in the house?"

"I saw someone there a couple of nights ago."

"Oh, the cleaning woman, no doubt."

"Ya, no doubt." All this only added to the confusion. He was sure that David must be mistaken. If David was mistaken, why was he told the house was empty? Who knows? Perhaps David was in on it too, then again, perhaps not. The next logical course of action was to talk to the cleaning woman. The next day was Monday. He would have to keep an eye out for her. At quarter past nine, the other guests started to arrive. David introduced Harry to so many people, that he soon lost track of who was who. David was quite a popular guy, especially with the girls. It would only seem right, based on that, that he would know if someone lived at 152 Brooks, predictably if it was a lady. In between introductions, Harry couldn't seem to stop thinking about what he had read in Dr. Harris' notes.

He also couldn't stop thinking about all of the strange things that had happened to him since he moved in. Over and over again he weighted all he experienced and came to the conclusion that David must be wrong. Someone did indeed inhabit 152 Brooks. It was all very unsettling. He was sure that David would never again invite him to any of his private affairs, simply because he had made a total idiot of himself. While David was introducing him to one of the female guests, he tensed with the sudden realization of one part in Dr. Harris' notes. Instead of thinking it quietly to himself he spoke his thought out loud. "Once in awhile she would whisper a name. The name was Harry." He immediately excused himself of course, but that did not alter the fact that it had been said.

This was the first night that he was to go to her, instead of her coming to him. This was perhaps the only way, or was it? He perked a pot of fresh coffee. It was two a.m. He thought at first that she wouldn't show, but soon realized that she would. He had been sitting by his window in the bedroom for half an hour, when the light in the tower window suddenly went on. Both of the windows were open so that he could see and hear everything that was said or done. He listened quite carefully, yet could not hear a sound, so he concentrated on watching. She was there all right. She danced over to the window and looked straight at him, yet she appeared to look through him. She caressed the curtain then casually turned to face her mirror. Apparently she was preparing for bed, as she unbuttoned her night robe and carelessly flung it onto the bed. She brushed her hair, one hundred strokes. He jumped suddenly, as if awakened from sleep, as the most telltale laugh issued from her mouth. A laugh of evil, or should it be said satisfaction. It was now that the air grew suddenly cold and a sick feeling arose from the very depths of his soul, for now he knew as well as she, that he was under her control. She whirled about violently to face him, with only two windows and empty space between them. She placed her hand slowly, firmly against her window screen, as if to touch him. A strange light danced in her eyes, burning into his.

"I knew you would come, my love. You couldn't stay away very long. You will continue to come, until I have you here with me, where you belong, but, of course, that will take time. As for me, I have all the time in the world. As for you, well, you haven't that long. For soon it will end. Soon my love, soon." The end of her laugh was followed by the sound of her breath extinguishing the flame of the oil lamp. His mouth was dry and burning, the rest of his body limp. All the same, his mind rejected. He couldn't comprehend what had just taken place. He jumped up in a rage, tearing at the window screen, screaming, "No, no, no. You'll never get me. Never. Do you hear me? Never!" He listened but there came no reply. All he could do now was wait, although, he was never very good at waiting. He rested his aching body against the window and soon fell asleep. Perhaps in his dreams, he would seek the answers to his questions, and this he did.

He was back again watching as though it were a play on the stage. It was early evening, a carriage rolled up in front of the house. A man descended and made his way to the house.

"Oh daddy! Your back. I'm so glad to see you!"

"And I you. Come shall we have dinner?"

"Yes, a nice, quiet dinner. Just the two of us."

"Did you really miss me that much? I find that rather hard to believe."

"I made up dinner special for your homecoming."

"My but you have changed. Has anything happened since I've been away?"

"Why? Daddy what makes you think that? Everything has gone on in the same boring way. It's just that I'm happy to see you, that's all!"

"Well, if you're sure that's all it is. Tell me what you did while I was away."

"Nothing much, just the usual reading, French lessons, and an occasional stroll around the grounds."

"You didn't talk to anyone, I hope! You know that I strictly forbid it!"

"Oh, no daddy! I wouldn't think of going against your wishes."

It was the next day. The sun was shining brightly. A messenger boy rapped loudly at the front door, which one of the servants answered.

"Message for Miss Brooks."

"Thank you. I'll sign for it. Miss Brooks, telegram for you here." Apparently she was out strolling, so the servant set it on the corner table in the front hall. She figured that Miss Brooks would find it upon entering. Dusk was slowly descending, as Mr. Brooks entered the house. He shut the door and locked it when he noticed the telegram. Presuming it was his, he carried it into his study. It read; Please meet me at seven tonight. Love Phil. He stood there as if trying to convince himself that it wasn't true. He knew that she had acted strangely ever since he had gotten home. How would she know that he had to go out of town again tonight, unless. He hurried over to his desk and sure enough, his papers were out of order. Strange that she would have left them that way. She knew that he would find out, if they weren't back in the order that he had placed them. Now he knew, it was too late. He rushed to the door of the study and bellowed for the maid.

"Sarah would you come in here please! I want to talk to you."

"Yes sir, what is it?"

"At any time while I was away, did Jessica leave the house?"

"Well, I promised her that I wouldn't say anything, but seeing how upset and all you are, then I have to admit that she did on quite a few occasions."

"How late did she stay out and when did she leave?"

"She left each time around seven thirty sometimes earlier and came back around midnight."

"Thank you Sarah! I'll see to it that you are well paid for your honesty this month."

"Thank you sir. Will that be all?"

"Yes, that will be all." Now he had all the information that he needed to be sure. The time was six-thirty. He had half an hour to make plans.

"Why didn't you tell me sooner that you had to leave again tonight? We could have spent the rest of the evening together."

"I didn't want to upset you."

"All the same, I try to understand and now I think that I do. After all, if you didn't have your job I wouldn't have such a nice house with servants to look after me and clothes to wear. So, you see, I do understand."

"I think you do and it's about time too. Whenever I had to go away, you used to carry on so that I hated to go. But now that you understand, I'm sure that things will change."

"Yes daddy, I'm sure that things will change."

"I must be going now. Be sure to take good care of yourself!"

"Oh I will daddy. Do you want me to come to the station and see you off?"

"No, that's quite alright I don't mind going alone."

"When will you be back?"

"Is it so important to know?"

"Not really. I was simply wondering when you would be back so that I could be ready when you arrived at home."

"It's rather hard to say, but at any rate I'll be back when I get back."

"But daddy, I really would like to know."

"I said that I didn't know. Now that's all I can tell you." She watched him enter the carriage and then proceed onto the street.

He carried out the first part of his plan by driving over to the telegraph office. Once there he sent word that he couldn't make the trip. Before he left the house, he had informed Sarah to keep the back door open. On the way back, her words ran through his mind and already hatred started to kindle in his heart. He got out of the carriage a ways from the house and walked, just incase she was still at home, which he doubted very much. He didn't want to make any mistakes, this was far too important. The minute that he stepped into the house, he knew that she had gone. She usually played the piano or had a

French lesson. Immediately he asked Sarah which way she had gone when she left, and how long ago.

"Well Sir, she left about five minutes ago and went towards town. That's all I know, Sir."

Jessica felt so free, so happy, so light. She couldn't wait to see Phil. She felt so at peace with herself, everyone, the world. She never dreamed that the time would come, when she would be walking down the street alone, in the twilight, going to meet the one that she loved. She enjoyed this newfound freedom. She never had this kind of freedom before, thus it was a new and wonderful sensation. She wanted to share her urethral feeling with Phil. There was no reason why they couldn't be free together. She felt that she could do anything that she set her mind to. She fancied that together, she and Phil could just leave and go anywhere they wanted to. She laughed gleefully at this thought. She didn't have any responsibilities to hold her here, just as she had no one she would wish to stay for. It seemed that she had waited for so long to find someone, who would notice how soft and lustrous her hair was, and who would tell her how beautiful she was. Every woman desires a man to notice her physical attributes and so thus Jessica was no different. The moment that Phil had kissed her and told her how beautiful she was, turned out to be as wonderful as she had fantasized that it would be. When it came time for them to part, she hated to leave the security of his arms. She vowed that someday soon she would never have to leave him again.

She had waited for years for someone to come and unlock the door to her prison, the prison that her father called home. He kept her there away from everyone and everything. She used to get so depressed, so discouraged. Then overnight her life had changed drastically. She fell in love and was in turn loved. To never of have experienced love in ones lifetime, would cause ones life to be incomplete. Her natural instincts to start a family of her own and make it secure arose within her. It was time for her to leave her father and to start her own family. She pictured the type of home that she would make for herself, her husband, and her children. She yearned for that so much. She just couldn't wait. It would be so wonderful to wake up in the morning in Phil's arms and to have been able to say goodnight instead of goodbye. All things in their natural course, it had come time for her father to let her go. He had done his job. His responsibilities for her upbringing were over, but would he let her go gracefully? She had found someone who made her feel special, different, unique. She was not going to allow her father to take her happiness away.

When she was away from Phil, she felt the pressure of everyday life and her father closing in on her. Now that she was going to be with Phil, she had not a care in the world. Without Phil, she wouldn't exist, didn't live, didn't thrive. When they were together, the time flew on swift wings, as if a fleeting dream. When it came time for them to part, it took hours for her to come down from her natural high. She knew that she would never be satisfied, till she could be with him twenty-four hours a day.

It was easy for her to describe the love that she felt for Phil and how it had changed her, but love is different for everyone. Love means and stands for many different ideals to different people. Love causes people to set goals and to go after them. Jessica had certainly set goals, in the name of love, and she meant to achieve them. Jessica's memory went back in time to when she had an intimate conversation with her personal maid. Apparently, it wasn't hard to notice that Jessica was in love. She had never glowed so much. Her personal maid was of one persuasion. She claimed that after having one lover after another, with no strings attached, she would never settle down and marry. Jessica did not heed what her maid said. She knew what kind of woman she was. Jessica could never be like that, never. She was in love and knew that she would never fall out of love. She would be faithful to her husband and be satisfied to settle down and be married.

He soon overtook her, but kept to the shadows as much as possible, for fear that she would see him. Half way towards town she met Phil and they walked together hand in hand to the park. Once there they sat and talked for about an hour. Then Phil mentioned going over to his house and meeting his parents.

"But Phil, suppose they heard all those things about my father and I. Suppose they have already formed an opinion about us?"

"Don't worry about it. I don't see how they could have. We just moved into town about two months ago. I'm sure that they would be happy to meet you. Come on, let's go."

"That's one thing my father is responsible for, do you notice how people stare whenever we go out into public places? Do you notice how they always whisper when our backs are turned? Well, I'm sure you can guess what they say. Aren't you ashamed to be seen with me? I'll never forgive my father for that, never!"

"How can you think that I am ashamed to be seen with you? Well, if I was, do you think that I would still go out with you and invite you over to meet my parents? Do you think that they would be so eager to meet you? Well, do you?"

"No. I guess not. Let's go then." If she could have seen her father, she would have known how she had hurt him with what she had said. For now, his face was twisted with anger and pain. All his life he had tried to make her happy and to protect her from them. He was afraid, afraid that they would take her away from him as they had her mother. He knew what he had to do. It was much more serious than he had thought it to be. His worst dreams were coming true, as he had prayed they never would. What bothered him the most was that he not only hated them, but his own daughter as well. If she had never gone against his wishes, none of this would have happened. Yes, perhaps he hated his own daughter more than the rest of them. He set off for home knowing that it would be some time before she came back.

"Thank you for a very lovely evening. I hope to see you soon. Good night!"

"Parting is such sweet sorrow, my dear Jessica!" She arrived at home at exactly twelve midnight. She waltzed in the front door bringing with her the essence of the fresh night air, for she was in love at long last. Little did she know that her life would end so tragically, even though her heart was filled with joy. Her thoughts were occupied by only one thing. It was as if she were in a daze. It only took her ten minutes to prepare herself for bed. The anger grew and grew inside her father, until he became a madman striving to kill what had caused him so much hurt. He tried to calm himself, but just the sound of their voices made the rage burn within his heart. She thought that he had gone, but she was wrong. Phil still remained underneath her window, for he was in love also and set on winning her.

"Jessica, my fair Jessica, tis I, your faithful prince. Come out so that I may behold your presence." She came peering out of her tower window clad in her nightclothes, holding an oil lamp to enhance her entrance. The moon was full and shining a languid, white light. The night was hot and still. He bowed in her sight.

"My queen of all queens, will you come out and dance with me?"

"I am sorry Phil, but the queen has retired to her chambers."

"What must I do, my queen to get you to come out? Must I climb the castle onto your balcony to receive you?"

"Oh Phil, stop being a ham, if any of the servants see me I'll be in trouble. You're just lucky that my father is not here, although I must say that your folly has touched my heart."

"Good. Does that mean that you will come out?"

Her father was in the hallway listening to every word that was said, remembering, always remembering, when he was young and courting her mother. As he remembered, the pressure grew, getting stronger and stronger by the minute, rising and rising, higher and higher still, till it could go no further settling in his head and pounding. As his head pounded, his eyes turned glassy, his body limp and cold. Still the anger and hurt remained. He wanted to eliminate that hurt and that was exactly what he was going to do. In a fury, he went into his study, grabbed his shotgun and stormed out the front door.

"Yes. You will leave!"

Her face that was a lovely soft, dove white had turned to a rose petal pink as she realized what was about to take place. Phil didn't seem to notice, nor did he care. He went on in the same old easy way, perhaps because he didn't know that her father meant business. He thought that the old man did it because he just wanted to scare him off. So instead, Phil decided to call his bluff with refusing to leave.

"But Sir, I have come here to see your daughter, not you."

It was while Phil spoke that her father suddenly saw his wife, his dear, lovely, faithful wife, standing in the tower window and the man that took her away from him beneath it.

"No! You won't take her away from me this time. Do you hear? Not this time, because I'm going to stop you like I should have the last time."

He shot without hesitation. Phil was flung violently against the house then face downward upon the ground, never more to move. It was too bad that she had to see the whole thing. She was a very meek person, but all the same she fled down to where Phil was to see if there was a chance that he could be helped. She was headed off by her father at the bottom of the stairs. She didn't like the look in his eyes.

"Daddy! No! Daddy please no!!"

Her protests were drowned out by the sound of a shot, so strong and powerful that it could easily mutilate flesh beyond recognition. As she fell to the floor, she was in great pain, great pain. She felt as if she were being torn apart, piece-by-piece. In his dream, Harry could almost feel the pain as if he was part of her and he was actually dying as she was. He could see her put her hand over the wound and he could feel the blood issuing forth. Blood that is the single life giving force. He could feel her gasping for breath, but the pain increased instead of ebbing.

Every time that she went to take a breath, the pain would come and stop it. After a few seconds, her breath would no longer come at all. Those few seconds seemed like an eternity, although they were surely coming to an end. He seemed to be looking out of her eyes. He saw everything going black. Tiny pinholes of sight out of each eye were quickly swallowed up by the blackness from around the edges. She tried to say something to her father, but he could taste the blood issuing forth from her mouth and speech was not an option. He could feel the life ebbing out of her, as she must have felt it. It started from her toes and continued to rise, draining every last ounce of strength from her body and mind. Now the pain was rapidly gaining in intensity. It was all over, her view of vision was only blackness and silence soaked into her mind. She was dead.

Her father just stood there for a second with a feeling of satisfaction, as he saw his wife lying cold, still, and dead upon the floor. He had finally gotten his revenge. Then he saw his daughter lying on the floor, it wasn't his wife. He threw himself upon her weeping bitterly, but his tears couldn't bring her back, even though they ran down his cheeks onto his chest smeared with blood, as everything was stained with the death of innocence.

"They had to take you too, didn't they? Why couldn't they have left you alone? No, it isn't enough that they took your mother. They had to take you as well."

After her death, Jessica's father fell fatally ill. The last he was seen was at her funeral. It was a damp, dreary, and rainy day. It held neither the joy nor warmth of the sun. It was a shame that one so young and beautiful had to be given up to the earth, to the ground, to the dirt. It must have been a nightmare lying in the coffin surrounded by darkness, by nothingness. Feeling the smooth, texturized sides of your tomb. Pushing and pushing with all your might, against the top, but your efforts are in vain. It won't move. You can hear muffled voices, but you can't make out the words. You try to yell, call out for help, but the sound won't come. It rises from the bottom of your throat only to become lodged within. Thus emitting no sound from the strained vocal cords. Then it comes suddenly, unexpectedly, the sound of dirt upon the lid, the sound of eternity, darkness, nothingness, and decay.

Her father was never tried for murder, partly because of his health, but mainly because it was proved that he was not mentally competent. He spent the rest of his days a broken man. A man with no heart, no feeling, no love. He spent his time staring into space reliving the happy times he had spent with his daughter, his long, lost daughter. She was an extension of himself, of his own flesh and blood. Why couldn't he have gone with her? Why? He knew that they wouldn't end it for him, so he had to do it himself. They pitied him, or did they? When Jessica died, his heart died with her. They should have been merciful and buried him with her.

When her mother left, he thought that he would grieve forever. His pride just couldn't accept the fact that she had left them for another man. An enemy from the outside world took his wife away from him and a mother away from his daughter. He failed to understand how she could have left her infant daughter. Surely, the mothering instincts in her should have been stronger than that of her own personal desires. Eventually, he transferred his affection for his wife to his daughter. Instead of just being her father, he was her mother as well. He took the loss of his daughter as a mother would. He felt as though, he had carried her for the nine months required for her development and went through the pain of bringing her forth into the world. He tried to shelter her from the unniceties of life. One of which was her mother abandoning them both. He came to the conclusion that he would create a safe, cheerful, and happy environment. An environment, which would not allow the outside world to enter. He didn't want the same thing to happen to his daughter. He would keep her to himself, all to himself. He had her selfishly for years, but once again his job allowed the outside world to invade his private environment, that he alone had created for his daughter. He had no choice, but to take the situation into his own hands. He had to eliminate the enemy from within his own environment.

He thought that he had won, but fate played a very cruel trick on him. Now he had time, only time, so much time to remember how Jessica herself had turned against him, hated him, loathed him. Everything that he did, he did it for her. She, however, did not see it that way. Perhaps she never really did understand. She thought that there was something wrong with herself or her family. She thought that he was being cruel to leave her home alone so often. She had become independent, too independent. He was missing from her life too much. She started not to miss him. She started to plan her days without him. She only depended on him to feed and clothe her. Soon, she intended to not depend on him for that. She provided her own piece of mind. But, for her own peace of mind to be complete, she needed to be loved and to be free. Free of her father's bonds. This he understood for he himself, at one time was young and desired the very same things. Being human we all desire these things. He merely wished to spare her the agonies of a love gone wrong. He merely wished to spare her the reality of finding out that there is never freedom for anyone, as long as responsibility exists. These lessons he had learned the hard way. He thought that he could spare Jessica a few hardships along the course of her life. Perhaps life has to contain a few hard knocks, in order to make one's goals all the more sweet for the taking. Perhaps, there are some lessons of hardship that cannot be taught, but must be experienced. He had felt ashamed, a failure. He had failed as a husband and now he had failed as a father. The only thing that he was good at was his job. No doubt, he was a husband and a father to his job, but his job could not give him the love and affection that a wife and daughter could. He felt that everything he had ever done to protect Jessica, he had done in vain. She did not appreciate all of the pain and worry that he went through to provide her with the best of everything. Then again, she never had the opportunity to view the poverty of the world. She could not draw a comparison. Perhaps, she thought that everyone in the world lived with the same comforts as she, maybe they would have been better off to be poverty-stricken. They would have enjoyed the simple things in life and treasured the few possessions that they had, maybe he would have still had his wife and daughter. He had to stop with the what if's. The fact remained that he had lost both of them. He had lost them because of his own stupidity, only he remained. He had lost what had made him superior to the others. He had lost his staunch will to survive and not merely exist. He had lost his stubbornness to enforce his opinion. Most important of all, he had lost his pride, the pride that his family had aroused within him. If he had youth on his side, he might have considered forging on, for he could have changed his status and mistakes in life, but now that he had only his money left, he had nothing! All the money in the world could not turn back time, so that he could once again be with his wife and daughter. Money, what good was money, when one had not love nor happiness? Oh! He had gone through a period in his life when he desired material wealth, but that was merely because he wished to keep up with the times and the higher classed, higher income people. He looked around him. All the material wealth that he had acquired within his lifetime, was gathered all around him. He felt as though it was closing in on him, slowly, very slowly. It would shut out the light and only darkness would prevail. Would this darkness hold comfort and warmth for him? An answer? Perhaps, an answer? Would that be the end then? Would he be doomed to suffer endlessly? He thought about how long this wealth would last, years beyond his going. He thought about all the years he had worked so hard to acquire wealth for Jessica. He had fooled himself. He thought that this wealth would bring Jessica closer to him. It would bridge the void in their relationship, but instead it only pushed them further apart. She required only physical comfort from the wealth that he had awarded her with. He knew that she would gladly give up everything that she had to be free of his dictatorship, his love.

He thrashed out at the medicine on the night stand, next to his bed. The medicine bottles shattered on the varnished, wood floor and the medicine slowly, surely seeped into the spaces between the floorboards, just as his consciousness, awareness, and life, slowly and surely seeped into the cold, meaningless, dense darkness.

Often there could be seen a light in the tower window, a small, dim light of an oil lantern. He died one night in his sleep, finally put to rest. Perhaps, he would find the peace and happiness that he had sought so long for in vain. He went to join his daughter, or did he?

Harry awoke drenched with perspiration and the feeling of an absence of someone who used to be there. Someone who was essentially just like him. This person ate, drank, and slept, but most important of all had dreams, dreams that were never fulfilled, never to be satisfied, never to be quenched. Pity, self sacrifice, and helplessness clouded the physical features of his face, for no one can really understand the concept of death. It seems so long and complicated to give life, yet so short and easy to give into death. One second you are healthy, happy, and alive, the next second your eyes glazed over with death. He knew as we all know that death is an inevitable fact of life. Yet, to those who survive and not merely exist, it comes what seems much sooner and too much harder to give into. A famous saying came into his mind "The good die young." How true this could prove to be, how very true. Suddenly, a wave of psychological cancer started to creep over his mind, a sure cancer that started to eat him alive, taking away his lust for life, and leaving the thought that it makes no sense to go on living. Nothing matters anymore, nothing matters at all. It seemed as though he had die with her, but no that couldn't be. It was nothing but a dream, a damned, bloody nightmare, from that moment on he had only one obsession, and that was to prove that Jessica did not and never did exist.

Leaving behind the dream world, he picked up the pieces of his daily, regular routine. He jumped up from the table and went over to the window. A red Volkswagen pulled up the driveway of 152 Brooks. Now, he was to put into effect the very intricate and involved plan of proving Jessica's nonexistence. A woman somewhere in her early fifties got out of the car and headed for the side door.

"Excuse me, you must be the cleaning lady?"

"Yes. I am."

"Would you mind telling me whom I could ask of the household for a job? You see I noticed the house could use a good painting, the lawn needs a mowing, and the flower beds could sure use weeding, at the moment I am in bad need of extra income."

"You would have to inquire with Mr. Harper at 110 Highview Terrace."

"You mean no one lives in the house?"

"Nope. I understand that it has been that way for years now."

He thanked her and walked back to the house into coldness, darkness, nothingness.

It began to rain late that afternoon and a cloud of depression weighted heavily on his chest. He felt so miserably alone. Even when he was younger, he felt alone at times, but not so completely. One could always jump in the car and go out to a movie or nightclub somewhere. The need to live another life was a grateful escape for those regular customers of the town theater, as he had once been. He would become so intertwined mentally and emotionally in the movie that his individual life no longer existed. When the movie ended, he was forced with regret and stubbornness to return to the lifestyle that he had come to know only too well. His attempts to have the movie linger on in his emotions and mind were futile. He thought of calling Cleo, but then decided against it. He didn't want to rely on anyone, for too many times his trust had been violated.

Lazily he turned off the news and headed for his bedroom, to curl up with a good book. It seemed impossible to get interested in the story. He tried so hard to escape his problems and depression by following the story along and not thinking of anything else, only it just wouldn't work. If only to escape for an hour, would be enough to see him through. He needed still more evidence to prove that Jessica was not real, but at least he was one step closer than the day before. He stopped reading and listened to the rain hitting against the windowpane. Everything was a light, ghostly gray, for darkness had not yet descended. The steady melody of the raindrops on the windowpane soon lulled him to sleep.

In a state of semi-consciousness, he felt a sudden chill, yet all was still, still as death. Warmth as of another body now caressed him, no longer did loneliness reign in its domain. He was not alone, as she silently warmed and caressed him to herself, as a mother comforts a child. He wanted to run from her and cower in a corner. He wanted to cringe from her touch, yet it wasn't as cold, terrible, and clammy as he had thought it would be. In fact, he didn't really mind it at all. He knew now that he had to stir himself from this world of half light and half darkness, or forever be cradled in her embrace. That is exactly what she wanted, wasn't it? She had almost succeeded.

He suddenly jerked his body and sat upright on his elbows. Everything was just as he had left it, the light was still on, his book upon the night stand, and the rain hitting the windowpane. There was something strange about the room though, something that his senses had not yet perceived. It jumped on him, quite unexpectedly, jarring back the memory of his world of dreams. The covers on the opposite side of the bed were slightly ruffled. Could it be that he had turned in his sleep? No, for he was in the same position when he fell asleep as when he awoke. The slight scent of lilac heavily loafed on the air, and when he leaned over toward the opposite side of the bed, the scent seemed to be stronger. Confusion clouded his mind and before he could clear it, lightning flashed and thunder boomed. An alien fear had grasped his heart and he had to face the unforeseen truth that she had been there. It wasn't a dream, it was real, just as the first night he stayed there and saw her was real. The lightning lite up the room sketching a maze of patterns from the trees outside on the opposite wall. He was frightened that she would come back again and he knew if she did he might just weaken enough to give her control. That is if she didn't already have control. He forced himself not to think of that possibility and thus avoided the consequences. As frightened and alert as a hunted animal, he refused to give in to sleep. He kept his eyes casing the interior of the room. He could no longer tolerate being in the bedroom and fled to the living room where he turned on the television and laid down upon the couch. Soon the television would go off the air and he would have no recourse but to turn it off, emitting nothing but silence. The night seemed to pass by so quickly, yet the evidence of fatigue wore upon his face.

Cleo Thompson walked uncertainly up the driveway, for she wasn't sure whether or not she had the right house. She glanced over towards the right and 152 Brooks loomed up before her. It gave her the impression of being empty, lonely, and deserted, an old house holding years of misty memories, some happy, some sad. It looked strangely haunting, preserved straight out of a gothic novel. She didn't care to learn of the secrets it enclosed for the thought left her suddenly cold, although curious. The knowledge that a house where people have lived and died is haunted gnawed at her from the dark recesses of her mind. Perhaps, this was why it held such a strange fascination over strangers. It had lived long, much too long and seen to many die under its roof, with their lives unfinished. Once up to the door, she was assured that she had the right house because she saw Harry's name on the mailbox. She knocked impatiently for five minutes. Finally, she heard a slight commotion inside. Slowly the door swung open and Harry blinked in the bright light.

"My god, Harry! What happened to you?"

"Didn't sleep too well last night!"

"I should have guessed." He thought for a moment that her saw a hint of suspicion in her eyes, but then it was gone. Who would believe such a feeble excuse as that? It wasn't so much that it was an excuse, just that there was more to it than that. He could just imagine what wild thoughts would run through his mind if he went to Cleos and she answered the door with disheveled hair, wrinkled clothes, and a haggard, worn, exhausted look upon her face. Worse of all he needed a shave badly.

"I'll fix some coffee while you go and shave."

A short interval followed while he nervously shaved, shaking as he was, he feared a cut would betray his condition. He didn't care one way or another whether he did shave to improve his appearance, just as it didn't matter whether he changed clothes. He did for the sake of decency and nothing more.

"Sit down and drink it while it is good and strong. Now what really happened last night?"

"I had a bad nightmare and couldn't get back to sleep because of the noise from the storm."

"You look like you haven't slept for a week. Are you sure that there is nothing else bothering you?"

"Like what?"

"I don't know! It's just that you have the look of a man who has spent all his energy on worrying. You seem so far away like you're in another world. You're just not yourself Harry, that's all."

"I'm still the same old Harry Cromwell speaking to you in the flesh. That you can believe."

"Can I have a tour of the house?"

"Sure, go ahead. I've got to take a shower and change my clothes." No sooner had Cleo gotten there than he was anxious to get rid of her. His mind revolved around the thought of proving Jessica never existed. He was at least one step closer, soon he hoped to be more than just one step ahead of the game.

He dropped Cleo off at her house and proceeded to 110 Highview Terrace.

"Good afternoon! I'm Harry Cromwell. Could I ask a few moments of your time, to speak to you?"

"Certainly, come in."

Mr. Harper was a well to do middle-aged man with graying sideburns at his temples. Harry felt ill at ease under his steady stare, for he seemed to be very particular in his own mannerisms.

"What can I do for you Mr. Cromwell?"

"It's what I can do for you."

"Oh, really! I'm interested, go on."

"I live right next door to your house on Brooks Avenue, and I was wondering if perhaps I could take care of the place a little. You know I could mow, rake, weed, stuff like that. I'm in bad need of extra income right now because I am going back to college in the fall. It seems that all of the other college students got jobs ahead of me since I had to take the time to move, now I'm behind."

"I see, Mr. Cromwell. I would be tempted only now I'm afraid that I have given up on the place. I've put too much money into it and got nothing in return. The house is just a jinx, I guess, for the people no sooner move in than they move out. No one stays long enough to pay two months rent."

"Then I take it that no one is living there now?"

"Correct and not for some time now, nor for a substantial amount of time once they have moved in."

"You're positive that no one would be fooling around in the place?"

"Quite, or else I would have heard about it from the housekeeper. Why? Have you seen someone prowling around?"

"Well, I thought I saw someone."

"Are you sure that it wasn't the housekeeper?"

"No. No doubt, it was just my imagination."

"Well, I'm sorry that I can't help you out Mr. Cromwell. Once in awhile I send one of the neighbors over to make the place look presentable, just in case someone does see the place and decide to rent. I would appreciate it though, if you could keep an eye on the place?"

"Of course, no trouble. Maybe it was the last tenant coming back to get some of their belongings that they forgot."

"I don't think so, Mr. Trent moved out in March."

"Harrison Trent?"

"Yes. Do you know him?"

"Yes, he is one of my college acquaintances. Thank you for your time Mr. Harper. Sorry I couldn't be of service." He thought on the way out that now he had more proof that Jessica did not exist. Still, he had seen her, perhaps she was sneaking around using the house. How could she go undetected for so long? The housekeeper goes in once a week, surely she would notice something wrong, yet no one but himself had noticed.

He knocked two times before his question was answered. Someone steadily walked up to the door.

"Harrison don't look so shocked. It's not the end of the world."

"Harry, old buddy, where have you been packing yourself away? Come on in and have a seat. It has been a long time since I've seen you."

"Ya, I know but time has a way of catching up with a person. Sorry that I couldn't get around to seeing you sooner, but I've been busy."

"You still at the apartment complex?"

"Nope. I moved to 154 Brooks Avenue."

"That's how long it has been since I've seen you last. We had our last class together all through first semester, remember? 154 Brooks huh? You know that I used to live in the house next to yours, 152 Brooks?"

"Why did you move out? We could have been neighbors."

"I didn't like the house. It gave me the creeps. If I had known that it would bother me that much when I first moved in, I wouldn't have jumped at the chance. I should have guessed that there was a catch to it somewhere along the line."

"Well, why did you move out?"

"I guess that you could say that I lost my nerve. The first strange thing that I noticed was the smell in my room. No matter how much I aired out the room, whether it was all day and night, the scent of lilac made me gag. Look, why don't we talk about something else. You'll think I'm crazy if I tell you the rest."

"Go ahead! I'll give you the benefit of the doubt. You got me interested, so you'll have to finish."

"Alright! I searched high and low for the source of the smell, but I couldn't find it. Finally, I ended up sleeping in the guest room for the rest of the time that I was there. You know, now that I think of it, everything seemed so trivial, but while I was living there I was constantly on edge. I couldn't sleep. Night after night, I would have nightmares. During the day, I would have to fight to stay awake. You know what would happen to me, if I fell asleep in Fat Jack's classroom. Exams were coming around and I had all the hassles that I needed to prevent me from studying, so I moved out!"

"I can't say that I blame you. I would have done the same thing. Are you sure that it wasn't crazy Larry, Ned, and Mike who rigged up the house for a joke?"

"Naw, that would have been hysterical for them, but they couldn't make me have nightmares, that's for sure! Sorry! I'd like to spend more time catching up but I have to run. My job is waiting and believe me with a boss like mine, everyone is on time." They walked together out of the house and to their separate cars, murmuring what they knew would be unkept promises to see one another soon. They drove off their opposite ways.

It seemed as if everything was back to normal, since he had seen Harrison. No longer did he feel deserted and alone. At least, someone else had experienced the out of the ordinary occurrences of 152 Brooks. Could it be that no matter who moves in, she chases them out? How could she stay there for so long and not be detected? No one is that good. Somewhere along the line, she must have left a clue. Perhaps at one time or another, she had lived in the house and instead of leaving had stayed.

He felt a sudden closeness to the house. He was sure that if it could talk, it would tell quite a tale. There is something sad about a house that no one lives in. In place of bright, gay, curtain trimmed windows, blank, hollow, darkened eyes look out in search of contentment. Contentment which comes from gay laughter, echoing from room to room the sound of children's merry voices, the smell of freshly baked bread floating on the air. But then there comes a time when a house either out lives it's occupants, or it no longer provides a home and shelter from the elements. Such is the fate concerning man's architectural structures. Yet, a house is not totally empty, it is filled with laughter and memories of yesteryear. It beckons pitifully to by passers. It uses the instinct of curiosity, which was more than once the downfall of mankind. It shared in the dreams of its new occupants, concerning the style of home that they wanted it to be. It lived their moments of glory and died in their moments of defeat, such a faithful companion is hard to come by. One has to only look into one's own backyard to find peace of mind, for is it not one's own dwelling that reflects the qualities and downfalls of one's character. Houses live on in time, after a countless number of people have entered and left it's threshold forever. They are left standing to reflect upon future generations, one of man's sad, temporary, once needed mark of material wealth, for wherever man has dwelt, there also will you find his dwellings. Upon the morrow Harry planned to do a little research at the town hall. If there was to be a clue found at all of Jessica's existence, it would surely be found there.

The house smelled strangely musty and old. Accordingly, he opened a window in each room. The midday heat poured in freely leaving the thought of a nice cool shower quite inviting. Now was the time that he dreaded the most, the time that he was alone. Facts, doubts, and hopes crowded his brain. The more that he tried to sort out his thoughts, the more confused he became. He felt like an old, worn out man. Even with the cool, refreshing water splashing down and around his back, he felt tired of everyday life. The passion to feel the innocence and freshness of birth burned in his heart. It didn't work that way. One could not just jump in the shower and come out feeling reborn, lately how often he wished that it would be that easy. Surely, to wish to be reborn is a sign of growing old.

Coming out of the shower was like coming into a different world, for twilight had begun to fall. The twilight made him feel uneasy for soon darkness would come, with the darkness would come the unearthly creatures who could not live in God's daylight hours. Those who were good, kind and always longsuffering would lay their heads to rest, for them it was just the close of another long days endless search for happiness and peace. There was an understanding between the balance of the spirit world, and thus the darkness was given over to the devil's reign. It had always been this way from the beginning of time. No matter how technologically advanced man has become, this ageless concept would always abide in his subconscious mind. Harry was no different from the rest, when darkness fell, he too huddled behind locked doors. He did not share in any nocturnal activities. No matter how technologically advanced man has become, making man's life easier though none the less complicated, still subconsciously his fear of darkness lived on.

It hit him suddenly, most unexpectedly, he had the strangest feeling that someone had been in the house, as he walked towards the bedroom this feeling increased in intensity. He entered half expecting to see a dark shadow crouched among the other shadows in a corner of the room. He peered into the shadows of the room cautiously. To his relief, there was no one there. He sighed and turned on the light. Heavily he dropped onto the bed. With his eyes closed, he started to relax. He was practically asleep. Poised like a deadly snake above him, the scent of lilac caused him to turn his head and open his eyes. There upon the opposite pillow a bouquet of freshly cut lilacs rested. It had happened again. She had been there or perhaps she still was. He had been a fool not to look the room over better before he entered. He grabbed the lilacs roughly and threw them into the wastepaper basket. He quickly entered the kitchen, sure that he would find the door unlocked. It shocked him to find that it was not. He sat in the kitchen chair saying over and over to himself, that he had heard no one enter the house. He was sick, sick of the confusion, which clouded his mind. His nerves were jumping and pulsating wildly, but that was nothing new. They had been this way since he moved in. He was too tired to think.

He retired with a blank mind, sleep came permissively. He lay in a dead, still slumber. He could hear his own steady breathing. The dream world opened its door to him. In his dream he was looking out of a window. It was hazy out, a fog slowly slithered along the ground. The rain came, it beat furiously against the window. He fancied for a moment that it might shatter. The lightning flashed and he instinctively covered his eyes. The thunder roared and he grimaced at its voice. The wind came and with its bony fingers grabbed a hold of the window and shook it most unmercifully. The rattling of the window caused him to press himself against it. He could feel the coldness of the glass against his hot, burning back, still the rattling continued. He turned around and pressed his hands firmly against the glass. He stared out of the window, to the world outside. The flowers were down upon the ground, never more to raise their gaily decorated heads up to meet the sun. Their bright colors were dim as the rain had caused their petals to be splattered with dirt, many of the stems were broken. They had lived such a short time, yet long enough to bring happiness and color into the dull, colorless lives of some who appreciated their presence. He looked at his hands. His knuckles were white with the strain of the pressure against the window. His fingers were becoming unbearably cold. He removed his hands from the window and the storm ceased. A rainbow formed a half moon across the sky. The sun's murky, yellow rays shyly penetrated the window. He looked out the side of the window and there she was. She was happily picking lilacs off of a large, overflowing bush. The scent of lilac filled his nose. Instantly he was following her, past the lilac bush and along a narrow, dirt path. Shortly, they came to a white picket fence. She obviously knew this place very well. She entered the gate and left him standing on the other side. He wasn't surprised to see two weathered, ageless gravestones. He was too far away to discern the names written thereon. She gingerly placed half of her lilac bouquet on the left grave. She seemed to ponder briefly and then turned and walked away, as she passed him her eyes teasingly stared into his. She laughed gleefully and suddenly the sun was brighter, the sky bluer, and the breeze fresher. He could feel expectation tingle through his body. He was no longer at the family graveyard, but back inside his bedroom looking out his window. The window was opened so that he could easily hear a car door close. He looked more carefully and saw Cleo. She must be coming to see him. He heard her knock upon his door. He turned form the window to answer the door and let her in. He turned from one wall to the next, but no door could he find. Still, her knocks persisted. He cried out to Cleo, yet no words could he hear. He knew he had cried out to her and he started to scream. Frantically, he ran from wall to wall, searching, searching for a way out. Calmness slapped him in the face, of course, the window. It was now closed tightly and though he tried and tried it would not open. The knocking had stopped and there upon the lawn stood Cleo and David. They had the most terrifying look upon their faces. He followed their stares up to the tower window of 152 Brooks. He too gasped, for he saw not only Jessica, but himself as well. Together they stood in the window laughing, with a far away look in their eyes. He stood at the window helpless. He knew what Jessica was thinking. He started to laugh too, then caught himself and stopped. He screamed at himself to shut up. He stared at himself in the tower window, it was like looking in the mirror, and tried to will himself to stop laughing. It was useless. His fingers twitched and he could feel his bed beneath him. Now he could see himself at both windows and knew that he still resided within his body. The laughter continued in the background and he could feel the deep sleep that he had fallen into. He must wake up! He jerked his head and slowly the outline of his familiar bedroom came into his sight.

He was once again back in the world of the living. Sleep, he mocked the thought of it. No longer could sleep hold any rest for him. He tried to think normal everyday thoughts, but somehow normal was no longer normal. He felt his flight or fight response clicking into high gear and realized that he would indeed fight. He had a sudden thought from which a plan formed, which would keep him busy all the next day.

The newspaper clerk was short, sharp, and clean. He eyed Harry suspiciously because of his request. Harry realized how strange the request would sound to him if he were the clerk. He sighed heavily as the clerk finally left him alone. He had a lot of microfilms to go through. With his fingers crossed for luck, he began his search. He couldn't even guess if the odds were in his favor. If luck were with him, what he searched for would be on one of the microfilms. The process was slow and tiring, for he had to train his eyes to read every headline as they slowly proceeded up the screen. The constant focused attention caused him to feel sleepy and dizzy. Three breaks and two hours later, when he was about ready to give up, he found her. All of his attention was on the screen, as he read he took down notes, while slowly the reality sunk in. The headline read "Millionaire Kills Daughter and Lover." The article described Jessica's death exactly as he had see it in his dream, only he knew more details than the article provided. What shocked him the most, were the three faces, that stared back at him, from the microfilm reader screen. He thought at first that he saw a twinkle in her eye, but he was extremely tired. One other strange thing he noticed, Phil looked vaguely familiar. The physical features of his face were more than just a dream or memory. He thought no more of it and took a copy of the page. He felt suddenly calm everything had fallen into place. Jessica was not alive, yet she had existed in the past. He still could not however explain why he had the dreams and encounters that he experienced. He was pleased with himself for the facts that he had just established, perhaps it was time to place his dreams in the dream world, and his experiences with Jessica in the unexplained.

He returned to his residence and went over the copies that he had taken of the newspaper article. With a cold chill, he suddenly realized how closely matched his dreams were to the information in the article. How cold and cruel bare facts can seem. It was hard to find the right words to do justice to the situation. There was one main fact screaming out of the article in every sentence, MURDER. It mentioned nothing of the fact that one so innocent and young should not have died. Cold, impersonal facts, are all that justice is based on in a court of law. Human emotion can be considered a hinderance to the resolution of a crime. How could one man separate his emotions from his intellect? Should not a computer act as judge and jury, no doubt the solution would be void of all emotion. What a strange world he lived in, where innocent people tell the truth and end up living the rest of their lives behind bars, circumstantial evidence. Where just as strangely, the guilty walk freely among society for the rest of their lives, expediential lawyers. A fair opinion can be drawn about a person based on their background. The real crime in any situation is if the person in question has a background that is not allowed to speak towards that persons character. This concept tends to aid the decent, law abiding citizen and hinder the criminals in society.

Once again he studied the three faces, which in turn stared back at him. Jessica and Phil made a nice couple, but there was something else very familiar about them. He made the connection. He could have easily replaced Phil physically, in both looks and build. It was ironic that they should both look so much alike. He wondered why it had taken him so long to discover the similarity. Could it be that somehow Phil was related to him distantly? With all of the years between them, could Phil be an ancestor of his? He felt nauseated, discouraged, and disheartened. He knew that Jessica had been dealt with unfairly in her life. He knew that she suffered the coldness and cruelness of others, others who were denied their happiness and goals in life, thus denying Jessica her happiness and goals. He knew only too well how people could be cold and cruel. He had encountered many of these people during his life, as a child he had grown up with the attitude of trust. He considered himself to be honest, loyal, and trustworthy. He knew it was more important for him to believe in himself, rather than be concerned of what other people thought of him. Still, the thought that there would always be someone who would believe him dishonest, disloyal, and untrustworthy shadowed this belief. It was quite often that the manner in which people acted caused him to lose faith in the human race. He failed to understand how some people could be unsympathetic in their manner of thinking or doing. Because he himself could not deal cruelly with others, he soon learned that did not mean anyone else would as well. He came to the conclusion, in the early years of his life, that there were many aspects to a man's character, to society dictates, he could not and cared not to analyze. Thus, man built his empire, and thus, sadly enough man would destroy his empire. To every end there is a beginning, to every beginning there is an end, life is simply a circle and nothing more. Harry had made his beginning in life, learned lessons the hard way, and no doubt grew himself to be a little cold and cruel. Sadly enough is the consequences of being born into a world where there are already thousands of cold and cruel people. People who have been hardened by the cold and cruel people who resided in the world before their birth. Perhaps he thought, at times that it would be better to be hardened by life, than to have to go through life constantly fighting to remain and be honest, loyal, and trustworthy.

The feeling of exhaustion overwhelmed him. He was tired of thinking for no matter how hard he tried to arrive at a conclusion to his situation, the further a satisfactory conclusion drifted from his mental grasp. There had been times in his life when he could sit down and think logically. He looked at the situation on hand from all sides and finally came to a satisfactory conclusion, but not this time. Any conclusion his tormented mind could come to was not satisfactory. His mind was plagued with doubts. He began to wonder, if he could ever think clearly or logically again. Shadows, the shadows clouded the sunlight, that which used to be clear and fresh had now become clouded and stagnant. Within the confines of his mind the one thought which haunted him the most, within the confines of the house, was the realization that he and Phil were each others double. Nothing could stop this thought, this realization from echoing and reechoing through his mind. To leave, to go somewhere else would not remedy the uneasiness of his body, mind, and soul. He couldn't just stop and start over. He was too bound by responsibility. Responsibility, a force so strong at times as to drive a young, sane man to death and insanity. Insanity? Is that what this trauma is leading up to? Had it already reached that point? Insanity? Would that explain the situation? Insanity? Is that ultimately the satisfactory conclusion?

He rose from his chair, his body numb as if in a state of limbo. His mind was the only part of his body that was functioning, radically functioning. It was moving faster than his body. It was moving ahead of his body. He crossed to the bathroom. Staring at his face, the haggardness, weariness, and lines of newfound age and worry jumped out at him. He seemed a stranger to himself. The face that he knew used to be relaxed, young, and serene. Perhaps, that was not the real Harry at all, perhaps, what he saw now was his innermost self. He tried to justify this claim. He reasoned that he had to act relaxed, young, and serene to survive. In order to shut out the unpleasantness of life requires a certain level of insanity, to reject reality is totally a form of insanity. He then reasoned that everyone to some extent is insane. His time had run out. The insanity had overcome him. It showed him his true self in the mirror. It pushed him over the line, which separated fantasy from reality. He did not know which he had been experiencing, since he moved. He wondered how long it would take for one to emerge as the victor. He felt that the odds were in favor of fantasy, everything that he had experienced since he moved, would be a bitter pill to swallow as reality. However, there was some reality mixed with the fantasy. Two facts existed, two realities, Jessica had lived and Jessica had died. She no longer walks among the living, but does that mean that she does not walk? He was just drifting down the same old avenues once again. Questions, always questions, never answers.

He reached into the medicine cabinet and took out a bottle of antihistamine. He had used this during his two semesters at college last year to guarantee himself a good nights sleep. He was fighting for a means of escape. He had found one. Sleep came, yet not a relaxed sleep, a dead, still sleep. Dreams came, yet not clear, whole dreams.

Feeling a pressure across his brow, he awoke. The sunlight was flooding the room with it's colorful brightness. He arose and stretched thoroughly relaxed from a calm nights sleep. Last night seemed a misty memory. He thought to himself that he was just dreadfully tired and that a good nights sleep had been the cure. He ventured out and into the kitchen. Opening first the front door, he sensed all of his surroundings. Everything seemed so natural, so sweet, so right. Logically he deduced that all things play a part in the circle of life. The grass was so green. The sky was so blue. The flowers were so bright. The birds were so gay. He even sensed his own relaxed calmness. He felt that he too was finally a part of the surroundings, part of nature, part of the circle of life. He felt that he was fulfilling a very important quest. He was finally drawing near to the end.

The breakfast that he prepared for himself was tasteful from beginning to end. It seemed that he hadn't eaten for days and every morsel was a delicacy. Another dark thought crowded up front, the old Harry was sneaking through once again. He thought of a condemned man eating his last meal. How tasteful that meal would be. To know that one is enjoying the art of cookery for the last time. The darkness of that thought faded as he busied himself with other trivia.

While washing, drying, and putting away the breakfast dishes, he constantly thought of Jessica, sweet thoughts. Like an inexperienced schoolboy looking forward to a chance encounter with the girl that he fancied. He chided himself for such imaginings, but all the same those imaginings were there. They were there to the fullest extent.

bread caused him to turn towards the window. A loaf of bread rested on the windowsill, cooling in the soft, light breeze that billowed the curtains out ever so gently. The curtains were a bright yellow. The whole room was a blur of colors, yet toned down with cleanliness. All was where it should be, all was falling into place. He felt strangely, vaguely at home, at peace, at rest.

He turned his attention past the kitchen. He heard a light, hearty voice humming a tune in the next room. He followed the sound. He entered into the sitting room. She was there arranging a lilac bouquet on the coffee table. She obviously expected someone to tea. A shrill whistle expectantly filled the air. He jumped like a frightened child. He went back out to the kitchen and a tea kettle was whistling upon the stove. He turned it off, setting the kettle upon another burner. He returned to the sitting room, unfortunately she was gone, no longer there. A huge, stone fireplace occupied almost all of the space on the opposite wall. The whole room radiated warmth. A very wisely chosen arrangement of furniture and wall paper made the room quite cheery, yet docile. A huge grandfather clock stood in a corner of the room. It ticked in unison with one which hung upon the wall. Tick, tock, tick, tock, the grandfather clock struck the hour of eight. He loved the chimney tune that the clock croaked out of its wooden depths. It sounded so familiar, so welcoming.

He heard a floorboard creak and he followed the sound. He went out of the sitting room and into a hallway. The hallway was rather gloomy, consisting of dark, rich colors. A coat and hat rack loomed up drearily upon one wall. He turned to his left and she was there, halfway up the staircase. She was looking at him and not through him as she had done before. He knew not where he was going next, yet he approached her halfway up the stairs. He knew and reasoned that she belonged there, upon the stairs, wearing a cherry red, velvet gown, trimmed in black lace. Her gown harmonized with the stairs, which were covered with a carpet of rich, wine red. Her hair seemed to flow on and on, a dark, rich, ebony black. Her skin was white, too white. Her fingers were long and expertly groomed. He dared not stare her in the face. He was afraid of what he might find there. The truth perhaps, no more fantasy, but reality. Knowledge? Yes, the knowledge that he sought. Her face was alive, very alive. The mouth so finely relaxed and shaped, so natural in color. Such a warm, sensual glow. He met her eyes with his. She was searching his thoughts. She was showing him love, gentleness, and care. The feeling of physical want, warmth, and possession evaded his emotions. He wanted her as he had wanted no one. Her eyes said that she wanted him as well and that she had waited too long not to be determined to get him.

Her smile faded, as she reached out towards him. He grew cold, suddenly cold. Where was the warmth that he had expected? Fear came to him in the form of doubt. He doubted, doubted his need for her. He drew away from her descending one stair down. He looked down at himself, for he was shaking. When he looked up, she was gone, gone again. He wrapped his arms around himself for warmth, for all was coldness, yes, coldness. His temper flared. She was playing with him. She was playing a game of cat and mouse. She was toying with his sanity, emotions, and security. He wouldn't allow it. He just wouldn't allow it. He held onto the rich, dark stained, brown banister, to steady himself, as he proceeded up the stairs, to the level above. A breeze ruffled his hair slightly from the right. He turned and entered a room. He had entered her bedroom, he was sure of it. Everything was lavender, a bouquet of lilacs rested upon the dresser. The carpet was purple, the canopy bad was lavender to match the curtains, and the walls were covered in lavender stripped wallpaper. Everything, everything spoke of a strong, certain personality. He crossed to the window, the tower window. He moved the oil lamp and gazed out. His house was right across the way and he could see his bedroom window clearly. He heard a muffled laugh. Turning around quickly, he sensed that she was there somewhere, somewhere in that world of cleanliness, neatness, and loveliness, not a wrinkle, nor a speck of dust could be found in the house, a land of perfection. Perfect, he was thinking while he started to perspire, too perfect. He ran to the closet, the carpet absorbed all the sounds that he made with his feet. Flinging the doors open, he expected to find her crouching in the corner. Instead, he found what would normally be in a closet. A neat row of finely pressed, clean dresses and gowns, all smelling of lilac and lavender. He heard once again a muffled laugh and turned towards the doorway. She was there, amusement played upon her face. This only made his rage grow. He moved towards her and she moved away. He followed her halfway down the stairs, where suddenly she turned to face him. He could see the longing in her face, in her eyes, mouth, and breath. His rage left him. He felt old, tired, conquered, so tired, oh so tired. She once again reached out towards him. He murmured, "Oh, but you are so beautiful, so beautiful," automatically his hand went out to meet hers. Just seconds before their hands were to meet, he once again felt cold. Fear invaded his mind. He wasn't sure that he wanted to do this. She nodded her head, no, for she sensed his fear. She reached further and faster, the pleading was mirrored in her eyes. They touched, grasped, and intertwined. Understanding presented itself to him. He began to relax and grew contented, for he was warm, so warm. He was wrapped in her warmth. It wasn't cold after all but gloriously warm. He felt his physical consciousness slipping away, but to where? One last thread bound him to his physical being, that he once was, that he had always been. He was too relaxed to panic while he sensed the change. He wasn't ready yet for the transition, he just wasn't ready. This wasn't what he had expected. He tried to fight it, to ward it off. Still he slipped away from himself and closer towards her. He willed himself to pull away from her. She was determined not to let him go. He willed himself to scream out his protest. He heard the scream, yet felt not the effort. His scream rang through the now empty, drafty, uninhabited domain of 152 Brooks. No longer did it consist of cleanliness, warmth, and loveliness, only the memories of what laughter used to be there. The two weather worn, ageless gravestones were no longer waiting. They were joined by a third.

Cleo walked up the path to Harry's house, as uncertainly as she had the first time, all was quiet, too quiet. She had felt uneasy about leaving Harry the last time she had been with him. She tried her best to be a good friend. She had waited to hear from him the next day or the day after. She had heard nothing, so here she was. Her footsteps rang out loudly as she climbed the steps onto the porch. She felt that she was the only person out and about, not another soul could be seen or heard in the neighborhood. She rapped loudly upon the door expecting Harry to appear at any second. Five minutes later she had the silly thought, that perhaps he didn't want to see her. She glanced inside through the door. She noted how everything was in order, almost as if Harry hadn't been there for a few days. The house didn't look lived in, perhaps Harry hired someone to do his cleaning, perhaps it was cleaned today and Harry went out in order to stay out of the way. It was all just too neat and clean for Harry. She looked at the number on the house to verify that she had the right house. She then ventured to the garage to see if Harry's car was inside. The garage door was locked. Peering in through the window she could just barely make out the shape of a car. Obviously, he had not taken the car when he headed out. She glanced over at the neighboring house, maybe Harry was visiting over there. He had mentioned that a bachelor lived in the house next to his and that he had attended a social party there once. Would it be rude to inquire next door? Still, she felt the urgency to do so. Something was wrong, she was sure of that. Besides, she was never one to care about what other people thought.

The door on the porch was open and through it she heard soft music. She knocked hoping that it would be heard over the music. David Garrison strode arrogantly to the door.

"Hi, I'm Cleo Thompson a friend of Harry Cromwell. I was wondering if perhaps he was over here? He isn't at home, but his car is in the garage."

"Gee, sorry to disappoint you! He isn't here. I haven't seen him in quite some time."

"Well thanks. I'm sorry to of have bothered you."

"Hey wait! Any friend of Harry's is a friend of mine. Would you like to come in and have a glass of wine?"

"Sorry, I never make it a point to drink and run."

"Who says that you have to run off right away?"

"Oh, I'm a big girl now so I make my own rules."

"O.K, so I'm a bit aggressive. Don't run off holding a grudge."

"A bit aggressive, huh?"

"Let's call a truce. Are you sure that he is not sleeping or taking a shower?"

"I don't think so. Everything was quiet in the house."

"Maybe you should go over and knock again. I'll go with you."

"Really, you don't have to trouble yourself."

"Oh, no trouble at all."

Upon reaching Harry's front door, David reached under the welcome mat and withdrew a key.

"Hey! How did you know that was there?"

"One of the most common places to tuck the spare key."

"Yeah, that's Harry, easy going, non-complicated, go with the flow type of guy. Last time we spoke he seemed not like himself. I haven't heard from him in a few days and wanted to stop over and make sure that he is alright. Call it woman's intuition if you like, but I feel as if something is wrong."

"Don't worry, I never argue with a woman's intuition, never. Shall we go in?"

"I don't think that Harry will mind."

They searched the whole house. Harry was nowhere to be found. David even remarked how neat and clean everything was and quiet, so very quiet, dead quiet.

"Funny that he is not here! I don't know where he could be."

"Maybe he stepped out for awhile!" They both felt his absence, strangely enough, an absence of someone who used to be there. Once out on the back porch, Cleo turned her attention to 152 Brooks.

"Perhaps he is over there?"

"No way. No one lives there. The place is deserted."

"It wouldn't hurt to look? Would it?"

"I guess not if you really want to, but your wasting your time."

David followed her over to the side door of 152 Brooks. As they stood there, the house seemed to overcast them, engulf them, devour them. Cleo nervously knocked on the screen door. Creaking its groan of protest it swung open from the pressure of her knock. They hesitated for a few seconds, hoping beyond hope that someone would appear or call out. Nothing happened, for all was quiet. Curiosity overcame Cleo. She stepped inside and cast David a sneering glance to challenge him into following her. He did follow, though for no particular reason, other than to make a favorable impression. They entered into an empty, drafty, and somewhat cobwebby room. The bright colors on the walls had faded, remaining as a reminder of livelier, happier times. They then proceeded into a room with a huge stone chipped fireplace.

Their footsteps echoed emptily through the house. Off of the living room, was a hall of quite considerable size. Cleo gazed up the stairs. She called out Harry's name, knowing that it was useless. Of course, there was no answer, nor did she expect one. They both turned their backs to leave. Cleo suddenly clutched David's arm.

"Did you hear that? I thought I heard someone laugh."

"That's ridiculous! There is no one here. It was probably the wind."

"Ya, your right, I feel a slight breeze. Come on lets get out of here. This place gives me the creeps."

Once through the door of 152 Brooks, out into the open air, they felt a pressure lifted from their spirits. The house held a very brooding atmosphere. What ever air it held left ones lungs stuffy and burdened to fill themselves with clean, fresh air, not the musty enclosed air of one such house as 152 Brooks. David and Cleo stood upon Harry's front lawn. Cleo was going to thank David politely and put him down when he made his pitch to get her over to his house for a drink and who knew what else. David was trying to decide which approach would work best on

Cleo. He needed the challenge of trying to persuade the hard to get type. He hadn't had that type of exercise for awhile. David and Cleo stood there in silence, still thoroughly baffled with disbelief that they had not found Harry. Harry was not in the immediate area, not in his house, nor 152 Brooks. Cleo and David were wrong. Harry was to be found in 152 Brooks. It was Cleo who saw him first. She had to stifle a cry. Harry and Jessica were both standing in the tower window, arm in arm, looking out at them, laughing, just laughing, the crickets and tree toads mixed with the teasing, taunting laughter.

Darkness was slowly descending upon 152 Brooks!